Between the Wolves
and the Sheep

JAX CORTEZ

Dedicated to my loving husband and daughter, and to all the men and women in blue, along with their families, who support the very difficult job they do.

ACKNOWLEDGMENTS

Thank you, God, for giving me another year to put thoughts into words, words into sentences and for helping me shape those sentences into a story that I hope will shine some light on what it means to be human.

I also want to acknowledge the people who inspired me to write this book. They are the unsung heroes, the never-complainers, the men and women who give everything they've got to keep our communities safe, yet they get very little in return. They are the first to be placed under a microscope and scrutinized when things go bad. They are also the last to gain recognition for the good deeds that are done, such as the Dallas, Texas protests in 2016. When officers were ambushed and shot, as people ran in the opposite direction and away from the line of fire, other officers ran into the streets showering with bullets to save those in distress; or the recent events in Vegas in which several off-duty cops risked their lives to protect concert goers when a madman rained the crowd with bullets, injuring more than four hundred people and killing fifty-eight lives. Most good cops like these do this all under the guise of just doing their job, and those are the ones I want to honor.

I also want to acknowledge the family members who support and love them. For every birthday, holiday, anniversary missed, to sleeping alone or changing plans at a moment's notice, they are the ones who live in the underlying shadow of sacrifice, for even if it's not openly stated, they know one undeniable truth— that an officer belongs to the community he or she serves.

Next, I want to thank my husband for all those sleepless nights he's had to go through, working extra jobs to help put food on the table. You've always encouraged and supported my dreams, even during times I've wanted to stop when things got rough. You saw something in me and wouldn't let me quit, and for that, I can't help but love and support you too, my true partner in all things. You may think your girls don't notice, because you never complain, but we do. Rain or shine, in sickness or in health, you get up every day and go to a job that doesn't always say, 'thank you'; sometimes, people treat you with disdain and you constantly have to watch your back. I could never do what you do, nor tolerate what you tolerate, walking that fine line between the wolves who want to devour the sheep, but every time I ask if you're sure if this is what you want to do, your response is always the same: "Yes. I want to do something that is bigger than myself, and even if I don't make an impact, I know that I'm contributing a small portion towards keeping the people I love, safe," and for that, I give you a blessing and a kiss each day, and send you off with a prayer, because I know you belong there. Not all heroes wear capes and utility belts. Mine wears Kevlar and a leather belt. For that, I'm honored and proud to be your wife. Thank you for coming into my life.

The Final Inspection

The policeman stood and faced his God, which must always come to pass. He hoped his shoes were shining, just as brightly as his brass. "Step forward now, policeman. How shall I deal with you? Have you always turned the other cheek? To my church have you been true?"

The policeman squared his shoulders and said, "No, Lord, I guess I ain't, because those of us who carry badges, can't always be a saint. I've had to work most Sundays, and at times my talk was rough, and sometimes I've been violent, because the streets are awfully tough. But I never took a penny, that wasn't mine to keep. Though I worked a lot of overtime, when the bills got just too steep. And I never passed a cry for help, though at times I shook with fear. And sometimes, God forgive me, I've wept unmanly tears. I know I don't deserve a place among the people here. They never wanted me around except to calm their fear. If you've a place for me here, Lord, it needn't be so grand. I never expected or had too much, but if you don't, I'll understand.

There was silence all around the throne where the saints had often trod. As the policeman waited quietly, for the judgment of his God. "Step forward now, policeman, you've borne your burdens well. Come walk a beat on heaven's streets; you've done your time in hell."

~Author Unknown

PROLOGUE

"Did he actually pour acid on her face so no one could identify her?" the veteran cop asked. He rolled out the crime tape behind the trees, forming a square perimeter to secure the scene.

The chill of the night caused clouds of mist to float above the heat lamps, which were placed in every corner of the crime scene, lighting up the tiny area. I looked around and wished they weren't there. I was cold and hungry as I thought about having cancelled my daughter's recital for this. I was sure Gianna was furious. I had cancelled so many times I had lost count.

"What do you think?" asked Lou. "Same one who did it last time? Looks familiar."

I loved Lou, but I couldn't help but feel annoyed with the questions. I needed some silence to survey the scene. A crimson trail of crushed grass led to the direction of travel. I shook my head. I could see how the hikers found the site. A body dragged in the dead of night made any crime scene seem sinister and primeval. I had seen many murder victims in the past, but this one was now the third of its kind. I cringed as I thought about the last two. Her face was a mess of melted flesh; her right eye had been hollowed out and her nose was a tiny nub. I saw burn marks on her arms, chest, and stomach. The violence of the encounter that led to this turned my stomach. I felt the urge to vomit but resisted. I couldn't understand how someone could do this to someone so young and innocent. This kid couldn't be older than my nine-year-old.

Lou snuck up behind me and whistled as he hinged his hands to his hips. "The media's gonna have a field day with this one."

"Yeah, I know, Lou. The media has a field day with anything worth making all of us look like a bunch of incompetent morons."

I had been stuck in the same nightmare for about a year now. I needed to find The Eraser, as the media had taken to calling him, because he liked to erase his victims' faces with acid. Now that we had a third victim showing the same acid burns we had a serial killer on our hands. The pressure from the community to get this case solved was going to be intense. News about this murder would lead to a new level of panic.

"I found the underwear!" Lou's partner said. He pointed to a dead log right in front of him. He leaned over to stab an evidence flag into the earth.

"Make sure the crime photographer gets a shot of everything," I yelled over my shoulder. "I don't want anything moved or compromised."

"You got it," he cried.

I got down on my haunches and scanned the area. The drag marks coming from the east entrance of the heavily wooded park showed impressions of two footprints in front of the marks, which meant there was only one perpetrator. I needed to find a clue. One act of clumsiness was all I needed.

"This one tried to fight him," called the forensics investigator. I rose and walked toward him. His gloved hand swept away a mound of leaves and debris that was piled over the deceased's legs. "Look at the broken nails on her hand," he said. Her hands were so tiny, no bigger than the size of my palm. "There's tissue under one of her fingers. Also, obvious signs of penetration. There's a branch protruding from –"

"I got it," I said. Seventeen years in the force, but nothing made me shudder like the mutilated body of a murdered child. I stumbled away from the crime scene, finding a distant tree behind. I threw up what was left of Gianna's lunch tacos. I could hear another officer behind me doing the same. I doubled over and spasmed until nothing but the burning taste of bile crawled out of my mouth. I leaned against a tree and pulled a handkerchief from my right pants pocket. It was one that Gianna made for me when I first joined the Crime Division. I read the inscription she had sown into it: *Forever in my heart.*

I wondered if that was still the case. Lately, her mind was always somewhere else. Gianna hated how much I threw myself into work. She resented it. Now, heaving behind a tree, I had to admit she had a point. Sometimes, I wished I could split myself in two. One part would keep my humanity intact, unaffected by the horrors I witnessed, while the other could remain numb enough to continue fighting the monsters that walked among us. It was those monsters that left me questioning my hope for mankind. They drove me to keep working.

~*~

"What happened to my body? I can see right through my hands! And what's that man looking at under all those lights?"

"You don't remember, child?"

"No. I remember a bad man took me, and then you came to play with me. I remember being with you."

"Then it's not worth remembering."

"Sir, where's my Mommy and Daddy?"

"Please, call me Azrael."

"Azrael, when can I see my mommy and daddy?"

"You will see them soon. But first we have to go away for a little while."

"Go away? Where are we going?"

"To a place where there will be no pain, no tears, and no worries, my dear."

"Will that man be okay? Why are some of the policemen throwing up?"

"The work they do is very difficult, child. They're hated by many, loved by few, and see many evils."

"Why would anyone want to have a job like that?"

"Because for most of them, it's their calling."

"Their calling?"

"They are called to protect good people in a world filled with darkness."

"Doesn't God do that?"

"Who do you think was the one who called them?"

CHAPTER 1

"But, why *can't* I?"

"Because I *said, 'NO!'* That's why!"

My eyes popped open at the loud shrills of my wife and daughter coming from the kitchen. I stared at the closed bedroom door a moment before pulling the bed covers over my head.

"Whose decision was this anyway? *Dad's?*"

"It doesn't matter who gets to decide. We're your parents and when we say there's no technology on this trip, we *mean* it!"

I pulled a pillow over my head, but that never worked.

"Then why does *he* get to take a cell phone?"

"You and I both know why, Vanessa. Your dad's job requires him to be on call *all* the time. So, stop pushing the subject and hand over the cell phone and the iPad. *Now!*"

I exhaled, kicked the sheets off my legs, and jumped out of bed.

"Now *he's* calling the shots around here?" asked Vanessa. "What does he know? He's never even home."

I reached for the doorknob and stepped toward the door. *Sleep is for the dead,* I thought. *Four hours of sleep is standard for any parent, anyway.* I exhaled deeply and placed my forehead against the door, bracing myself for battle. This must've been what seemed like the third between my oldest and her mother over this camping trip. I loved this kid, but I knew we were in for a good run the moment she came out kicking and screaming. Some kids decide early on whether they want to make your life a living hell or an easy stroll through the blissful park of life. I thought about my poor wife. I supposed I couldn't blame her for waiting so long to decide if she wanted my demon spawn, as she liked to call it, when we got Vanessa.

"I *hate* you," I heard through the door. "You've *ruined* my *life!*"

Screw it! I thought. I knew it was cowardly, but I was the one who pulled a double last night. I jumped back into bed and yanked the sheets over my head. This seemed like a better trade-off than a full-on blowout. Gianna would say that Vanessa and I didn't get along because we were so much alike, and I supposed she was right. But I reached my zero-tolerance level for bull crap after dealing with local perps the night before. Today was not the day to mess with me. Any other day, maybe – but not today. I only hoped Gianna could forgive me for not being willing to volunteer to be knee-deep in drama just another day. Not that it made a difference. Except for Christina, everyone around here treated me like a leper. No one around here really listened to a word I said, anyway.

I heard muffled arguing through the bed covers. This time I had stacked two pillows over my head, but the match continued. Debating slowly turned into muffled shouts. I could tell they had taken the argument into another room. I let out a sigh of relief. I loved my kids, but

I missed the days when nothing in the whole world mattered other than my wild nights with Gianna, running around our tiny one-bedroom apartment, butt-naked, sipping wine in front of the fireplace and doing the dirty like a couple of wild rabbits all night.

Suddenly, the shouting stopped. I hoped it was over. Man, I missed Gianna. Her lips. Her smile. Part of me wanted to call her and tell her to slip back into bed so we could hold each other as she looked at me with longing. I loved the way her Latin brown eyes would sparkle when she would look into mine. I missed seeing her smile. It crushed my soul not to see her happy. I didn't care that she got more curves as the years went by, or wrinkled with the passing of time. What bothered me was how the temperature in the room changed whenever I'd walk into it and she was already there. She used to be so nice, so full of life, and now all I got from her was silence and disdain. I wondered what the hell happened. Where did I go wrong? It was as if we had spent the last seventeen years of our lives just going through the motions and learning to tolerate each other. Things were not the way I hoped. I wanted to be the knight, not the ogre. But instead, I felt more like the mutant reject. I knew my job had a lot to do with it. I had let work get in the way of my family. Problem was, I just didn't know how to fix it anymore. It wasn't like I could just walk away from my job. Everyone in the house depended on me to provide. Besides, my job seemed to be the only place where I felt some sense of respect and pride, nowadays. The downside had more to do with the temptations. I knew plenty of civilian women at work and in the field more than willing to open their legs at the sight of the uniform. I could probably ride them one after the other like a teenager in an amusement park if I wanted.

If I could signal anyone out, it would be Bethany – a side of trouble with a dab of poison. A ring on the finger meant nothing to her. She had a backside so tight you could bounce a quarter off it. She looked at me with hungry eyes, just the way Gianna used to. But at the end of the day, I needed to be able to look at myself in the mirror and be okay with what I saw. What type of pervert would I be if I tapped that? Sometimes when I looked at her it was like looking at my oldest. How could I face my kids if we fell apart because Daddy couldn't keep it in his pants?

No, I could never start anything with Bethany and I could never quit my job. I couldn't give up on my family. Gianna kept telling me we didn't connect anymore. That was why I was excited about this camping trip. I hoped being out in the middle of nowhere would do us all some good. But hope alone was never enough. In the end, I knew there were no guarantees.

Suddenly, I felt the mattress shift. I looked out from underneath my pillow. Nothing. I let out an exhausted breath and dropped the pillow back on my forehead. Then, out of nowhere, I felt the weight of an elbow plow into my gut, followed by the loud shriek

"*Kapow!*"

"Daddy! Daddy! I got you with a piledriver," chirped Christina.

Still trying to catch my breath, I rolled my nine-year-old toward me and cradled her knee to her forehead.

"Oh yeah!" she said. "Take *that*. FREEZE RAY!" Her tiny knuckles wrecking-balled into my nuts.

"Son of a–"

"*Mom!* Daddy's swearing again," yelled Christina. She slipped off the bed and disappeared out the door. Behind her flapped a red blur – what appeared to be a Supergirl cape. A wave of nausea swept over me like a dark cloud, packaged in a bundle of pain and weakness.

She sprinted back in the bedroom a moment later, dove into the bed, and gave me a great big hug. "Daddy, daddy, I'm so glad we're all going away together."

I gently shoved her off me. "Christina Maria Johnson. What has Daddy told you about hitting him in the privates?" I sorely regretted teaching her how to punch and where.

"Sorry," she mumbled. She casted her big brown eyes and porcelain face to a spot on the mattress. My heart melted.

"Come here," I said. I reached for her torso and squeezed her tight.

"Daddy, you're my hero," she squealed.

How I loved to hear those words, even if they came from only one member of the family.

Out of nowhere, Gianna's head appeared in the doorway and shot me the death stare.

"David. Phone call," she said. She turned and disappeared. Those words never meant good news.

I reached for the receiver and braced myself for the inevitable. "You know I'm on vacation with my family and there's no freaking way I'm coming in today," I said before hearing a voice on the other end.

"Detective Johnson? Hold on there, Tiger. So sorry to call you, but the chief needs the case file on that girl those two hikers found last month and we can't seem to find them. We have the other two case files, but we need to follow-up on a lead written on the last report. I'm afraid it can't wait."

I exhaled again and placed the receiver on my forehead. It was Bethany. Out of all the days to get a call back, this one had to be it.

"Listen, Bethany. They should be in the file, in alphabetical order like they–" I paused a moment and remembered I left them in my study. I had been reviewing the reports two nights before. *"Dammit!"*

"Aw, you remembered you have them, handsome? Well, now you're gonna have to get your nice little butt over here and bring them to me before you leave. I knew you couldn't leave without saying goodbye."

I heard the phone slam. But something was different. The noise of the house had vanished. Everything suddenly sounded much clearer. Then I realized. Gianna had been listening on the other end. *Crap!*

CHAPTER 2

I hated the forty-minute commute back home, but after briefing the detective in my task force, who was going to fill in for my case, maybe the long car ride would help buy me enough time to compartmentalize those vivid pictures of the case into the *Forgotten Zone* of my brain. But it didn't seem to work this time. I had memorized the words and phrases scrawled on the whiteboard in our office: *Three girls. Death by asphyxiation. Acid burns to face and body. Sexual assault with a foreign object. Torture. Sodomy.*

Those words hit me in flashes, sometimes even when I slept. The Eraser was still at large, and up to this point all we had was a loose cap. I was the one who had found it, behind the tree I had tossed my tacos into. We found traces of hair that our department sent to forensics, and it would take weeks to get it back. I clung to the hope that this was not circumstantial evidence. This last victim fought back. I needed them to find traces of his DNA underneath her fingernails. We needed a match. We couldn't rely on just the hair. But most of all, I needed to feel like my team had made some headway in this case. The story was already hitting newsstands and the whole community was in a panic. The media was doing its part; churning out stories that fed into that panic every day of my existence. The day of objective reporting was long gone. Nowadays they ran with anything sensational to gain attention. Every headline in the Lodge City Times detailed evidence of incompetence by our department. One reporter, Jimmie Zack, a self-proclaimed advocate of the people, ran an incendiary column called *Jimmie Zack's Got Your Back*. It was nothing more than the mindless rants of a sleazy, biased reporter, whose narrative specialties included race-baiting and baseless accusations about police brutality. He had been a pebble in my shoe since this whole thing began, and now that I was leaving town for a few days I was glad to be rid of him.

What mattered most to me was the importance of bringing closure to the families who had lost their little girl. I couldn't imagine the empty void I'd feel if something like that happened to one of my own girls. I imagined it was the not knowing that would probably keep me up late into the night, leaving me with an unsettled panic in my chest. The media couldn't understand this, or at least tried not to. They profited by churning up conflict, and this meant dragging a story about the murder of a child through the mud, all at the expense of the people hurting the most.

The only way to end the media hype was to catch this guy. I needed him to get clumsy. Just one mistake was all we needed. To this point, all we had to go by was a pattern. This one loved to dump the bodies at the local state parks that bordered our tiny, sparse city. America's hidden treasure of Lodge City, Texas had quickly gone from a retiree's dream to a law enforcement officer's nightmare, all in a span of one year. Deep piney woods, cypress and mesquite trees, rolling hills, rivers, and ancient caverns surrounded the perimeter of the city, all just fifteen to thirty miles away in any direction. The last three victims had been found just east and south of the city, still close enough for our sheriff's department to hold jurisdiction. My hands gripped the steering wheel tighter as I drove, thinking about how he took the lives of three little girls as young as Christina.

The thought left me craving for a good, hard cold drink. I reached for my glove compartment to take out my silver flask; a small sip before I got home would help numb the pain. It wasn't cold, but it would beat the cold stares Gianna flashed my way every time I reached for the liquor cabinet to pour myself a drink. I pulled out the flask, twisted opened the cap, and poured the contents down my gullet. *Dammit!* There was nothing but a drop of Wild Turkey on my tongue. I guessed I forgot to refill it the last time I arrived home late. Gianna hated the long hours I was putting into this case, but I made a promise to myself that he wasn't going to do this again. After that I had no choice but to catch him.

I pulled into the driveway two hours behind schedule. I saw my best friend Mike helping Gianna pack the trailer. She wore a pink tank top with black yoga capris, and carried a glass of water in her hand. She handed it to Mike as he loaded the last bin of what looked like camping cookware, onto the flatbed. She really knew how to wear those pants. They were greatest invention known to mankind in my book. If I could kiss the feet of the man who invented them, I'd do it. For a split second, she looked happy. I saw what appeared to be a wide smile as she leaned in to say something to Mike. She had the type of smile that could light up a whole room the moment she walked through the door. I longed for the days when her smile was all I could see.

But a moment later her smile vanished, just as she saw me pulling into the driveway. I felt my ego deflate as a scowl covered her face. I guessed she still wasn't over that phone call I got from Bethany. I wasn't looking forward to the half hour drive into the woods, her giving me the cold shoulder the whole way. This was not how I wanted to start my family vacation. I parked the sedan in front of my truck and unloaded the vehicle.

"Well, look who finally decided to show up," said Mike. He leaned in and did the half bro-shake, half slap in the back. He was a barrel-chested, wall of a man, and I felt the wind knocked out of my lungs when he pulled me in.

"Yeah, sorry I'm late," I said. "Thanks for letting me borrow your trailer. Good thing I told the girls to only bring the essentials. Otherwise, we might've needed two."

He chuckled. "Don't sweat it, man. That's what friends are for. Besides, once you become lead detective, I'm sure you'll have enough to buy yourself a nice, little RV. I know whose door I'll come knocking on to borrow that."

"Lead detective?" Gianna said, her eyebrows furrowed.

Mike saw me grimace. "Whoops," he said.

"You applied for the lead position?" she asked, hand at her hip. "When were you planning to let me know about that?"

I felt the color drain from my face. Mike had a puzzled look on his. *Shh...it!* I was hoping to break this to her gently once we got back from the trip.

"Gianna, I was going to tell you but–"

"When? When you were knee deep in cases and paperwork? Or when you're calling me to let me know you can't make our kid's next recital because you have to pull an all-nighter." Then she shook her head in disappointment and stormed back into the house.

"Geez man, I'm sorry. I had no idea, bro."

"It's alright, man. It's not your fault."

"Look, I didn't mean to cause a rift or anything."

"Nah. Fact is, things have been festering between us for a while. Don't sweat it. She just needs a little time to cool off."

But I knew that wasn't true. Leaving her alone was only going to give her more time to think about the 101 ways she was going to slice me into little pieces with her tongue about what a crappy husband and father I was.

"There's always counseling, bro. You have a beautiful family. I don't want to see the two of you fall apart, you know?"

"Counseling?" I laughed. "And what? Have some shrink tell me what I already know? That I'm doing a lousy job too?" I loved Mike, and I knew he loved to help. But I didn't want some stranger arm-chair quarterbacking all the mistakes I was making as a father and husband.

"David, I know you. You like to handle everything yourself. But sometimes we could all use a little help, man. Cindy and I were having some problems awhile back, and we worked it out. Counseling helped. If you need his name, I can give it to you. Just think about it?"

I nodded dismissively. "Alright, man. I'll let you know."

~*~

I slipped into the bedroom to assess the damage. Gianna shoved her clothing into a backpack with so much force, I thought she was going to rip through its bottom. I hated to see her angry, but a part of me loved the look of her flush, red-brown skin when she was. It was that fiery look on her face that she inherited from her Mexican-Italian parents that I found most attractive. She carried herself with passion, no matter what she was doing. It was the complete opposite of the tomato red look on my pale cheeks.

"Gianna?" I inched towards her. "We need to talk."

No reaction. We were officially on Phase 2: Stonewalling. I thought about reaching for her, but I knew that would be like reaching for a cactus that pricked back and stung, causing her to push me away. I wasn't ready for DEFCON1 mode quite yet.

"Listen. I know I didn't mention this earlier. I just wanted to wait until after our trip."

"I want a divorce," she said, without looking up from her backpack.

I knew what I heard, but the sound of it sent me into a tailspin of confusion.

"Did you hear me? I want a divorce. I'm *done.*"

They say that when you're on the verge of death, you can see your whole life flash before your eyes. This wasn't death. But I think I would've preferred the blast of a bullet between the eyes at that moment. Suddenly, a flood of memories played back like a reel on a black-and-white movie. I could see my beautiful wife's face when I first met her at a Warrior Run, soaked in fresh mud; then I saw the image of kissing her passionately in the back seat of my old Camaro while listening to "Open Arms" by Journey on the retro station, followed by spinning her in circles on our first wedding dance. Those memories moved to comforting the cries of my little girls as I rocked them to sleep on the day they were born, promising to protect them forever with every last fiber of my being. Memories... now...quickly fading away and dying; all from the simple cold, hard sound of those four little words: I want a *divorce.* I should've refilled my flask.

CHAPTER 3

A thirty-minute drive to our campsite felt like an eternity when driving in stone cold silence. Vanessa tuned us out with her iPod and headphones in the back seat. I guessed she had negotiated a tenuous middle ground in which she was allowed to bring some type of technology with her as long as it remained in the truck. I looked through the rear-view mirror. I could see Christina playing with her Supergirl and Wonder Woman dolls. She looked up and flashed what she called her explosive smile: eyes slammed shut, teeth fully exposed, chin up in the air. I smiled back. I glanced at Gianna next to me and reached for her hand. She recoiled, crossed her arms, and turned away from me to face the passenger's side window. After a few minutes, she pretended to sleep through the ride the rest of the way. I drew in a deep breath. I knew she was faking because she always fidgeted when she slept. I had grown used to the movement of her body, the sound of her breath, and the smell of her hair. I'd probably never admit it, but it lulled me to sleep. Not even a glass of Jack Daniels on the rocks could do that. I nodded my head. We used to be so close. How did things get so out of control? Maybe she was right. A short camping trip wasn't going to fix anything.

As I drove, I recalled the conversation we had right before we left for the campsite:

It's taken us seventeen years to get to this point, David. You're deluding yourself if you think one little camping trip is going to put the pieces back together.

We had arguments in the past over my emotional detachment from the family. They quickly disintegrated into her screaming, crying, and begging. Eventually, we'd work things out, and things would get back on track. But now she wasn't crying. She seemed cold and hardened, her words more unsettling. I guessed I took for granted that her complaints meant she'd always want to keep fighting for our future. But now she seemed more determined in her decision, even at peace with it.

"Gianna," I whispered as I drove.

She opened her eyes and glanced at me

"Think about what this is going to do to the girls. They need their father."

She shot me an incredulous look.

"What father, David?" she whispered back, emotionless. "You're *never* home. I'm their dad *and* their *mom*. I gave up *everything* to help advance your career, and you've done nothing but treat me like your personal assistant and full-time nanny, at best."

Ouch! My wife could be the sweetest person in the world, but when her tongue got loose, she really knew how to slice me in half with it. I threw a cautious look at the rear-view mirror and hoped that the girls were distracted enough not to listen in. I shook my head, took a deep breath and gripped the steering wheel even tighter.

It seemed we were going around in circles having the same conversation we had back home before we left for our campsite. That must be what insanity felt like. We were doing the same thing again and again and expecting a different result. I remembered telling her when I followed her into the bedroom after Mike left that I never asked her to stop going to school. That she had made that decision on her own. But all I got were scoffs and eyerolls followed by,

"And who do you think was going to take care of the girls when you were out playing *cop*? Did you think they were just going to raise themselves with *both* of us chasing down dreams?" She stepped forward into the bathroom. I followed close behind her.

"Look, I know this hasn't been easy for you. You feel taken for granted. I get it. I'm sorry I haven't always been there. We both knew this job wasn't going to be easy, but we have to work this out."

I could see her lean forward on the bathroom sink, head bowed and shoulders slouched. I couldn't tell if she was thinking about what I was saying or ignoring me.

I remember repeating the words, "I can *fix* this... I *know* I can. We can go to therapy. I have some accumulated time off I can take from this case."

"Ha!" She only rolled her eyes and threw her head back. "This case is *all* you think about," she said. "Or has it been Bethany all along?"

I knew she was going to bring Bethany into the picture. I felt exhausted having to reassure her that there was nothing going on with me and that girl. But all I got were crossed arms and a raised eyebrow. I hated when she'd look at me the way I looked at a perp who was feeding me a line of bullshit. Suddenly, I felt like I was the one being interrogated. I felt beads of sweat on my forehead. I'd be lying to say I didn't have an indecent thought about this woman, but I didn't *do* anything. Why did she have a way of making me feel like I was *cheating*? Why couldn't she understand that I *had* to drop a file to a very important case?! This had *nothing* to do with her. I lost my temper and yelled back,

"What the *hell's* wrong with you?! I'm busting my ass trying to provide for all of you—" In retrospect, this seemed to incense her even more.

"Don't you *yell* at me," the shrill sound of her voice sent shivers down my spine. Her eyebrows arched and she took a step forward, shoving me to one side as I stood in the doorway. Then, she uttered the final death blow—

"Get out of my way. I can't *stand* being in the same room with–"

"Mommy? Daddy? Why are you fighting?"

Christina appeared from behind me. Then Vanessa ran into the room. She looked at Gianna, who had tears in her eyes.

"Mom, what's going on?" Vanessa asked.

"Nothing's wrong, honey," said Gianna. "Just take Christina and finish packing, please."

"But—"

"Do it *now*!" I yelled. Vanessa flinched. I instantly felt like a turd. I hated raising my voice, but I only had patience for one dramatic episode at a time.

"Come on, Christina," Vanessa said to her younger sister. "Mommy and Daddy need to talk." She grabbed Christina by the hand and led her out, but not before casting me a bitter scowl as she slammed the bedroom door.

Gianna moved to the side of the bed and sat down. I sat next to her and reached for her. She pulled away and I let out a deep breath. Nothing frustrated me more than feeling like I couldn't reach her. This time I would plead.

"Look, things are really heated and tense right now. If you want the divorce, there's nothing I can do about changing your mind. All I ask is that we take some time to get away and really think about it before we make a final decision that is going to completely change the lives of our girls."

I waited for her response. She looked tired. Defeated. It broke me in half to see her so unhappy. I knew love could hurt. I just never expected it to hurt all the time. I wanted to reach for hand, place my arm around her and cradle her to my chest, but I couldn't. She sniffed. I thought I saw a tear run down her face; and finally, she nodded in agreement.

Perhaps she was right; it did take us seventeen years to get to this point. How was one little camping trip going to put all our broken pieces back together? I didn't have the answer to that, but I was damned if I was going to let this ship go down and burn without trying.

~*~

Getting away for an extended period was impossible with my caseload, especially during a high-profile case. Lucky for us, the state parks bordered our small city, just far enough for us to get away, but close enough to get back home quickly if we needed to.

As the buzz of city life slowly blurred and faded behind us, we began to see tall pine trees, rolling hills and outstretched, long gravel pathways. I could only hope we could somehow find a way to pick up the pieces and work towards clearing up the misunderstandings and resentments that had built up and festered over the years. Telling me that I had been playing cop really made me angry. I hardly considered putting food on the table and a roof over our heads *playing*. But there were some things that were better left unsaid. I'm sure she'd have a great comeback. After all, how could she really be happy running the homefront, cooking, cleaning, accounting, and caretaking for free all these years when I was always rewarded with a salary and work promotions? I couldn't help but feel responsible for getting in the way of her dreams all these years. I'm sure she wanted more but settled.

We finally reached the state park. The site opened to a circular driveway that led to a large cabin clubhouse. To the right, another dirt road led to an open campground about one hundred feet away from the lodge. A heavily wooded area surrounded the grounds from all directions. We arrived just as the sun began to make its slow crawl toward the horizon. Dark clouds loomed over us and a cold breeze swept in the smell of moistened dirt. Great. Rain. The last thing I wanted was to get caught in the rain.

"We're here!" Christina cried as she bolted out the door the moment I parked. She wore her red Supergirl cape, which was a blur behind her. I could see her dancing in mid-air as she ran into the field across from the site we always chose.

Gianna called out from her window. "If you can't see us, I can't see you, honey. Don't stray too far."

I looked over my shoulder. "Vanessa, watch over your sister. Your mom and I need to set up the tent." I got out and unloaded our things from the bed of the truck. She rolled her eyes and stepped outside, slamming the door.

I turned to Gianna and shook my head.

"Hormones," she said, as she stepped outside.

I didn't know if it was the sun setting behind Gianna, but her skin glowed as she walked to the back of the truck bed to pull out the tent bin. I wanted to tell her, but I didn't have the words. I reached for her hands once again, only this time she let me.

"Please, let me help you with that," I said. I couldn't believe that after all these years, she could still make my stomach leap when I felt her soft, warm skin. On the other hand, she seemed unaffected by my touch and moved on to the other items on the trailer.

"Look, Vanessa, *lightning bug!*" Christina said in the distance as I drove the corner stakes into the ground. I felt the edge of the vinyl tent and began to pitch the roof. I was a little rusty, but I still held the record for setting up the tent in under ten minutes.

"Stay in the open field," shouted Gianna. Her voice had a way of carrying across a distance when she wanted. It reminded me of the way I could make her squeal and yell when we'd make love. I smiled and watched her. I couldn't even remember how long ago that was.

I slowly shoved the sleeping bags, pillows, books, and night lamps inside the tent. The sky turned from bright gold to grey, warning us of the impending nightfall. Right now, I'd be sorting through my case files and getting ready to conduct follow-up interviews if we were home, all while my family prepared to sleep under the cover of darkness, blissfully unaware of all predators that came out to play at night. I supposed that, in some ways, I felt like I played a part in keeping them safe, protecting them from the hard realities that existed. They knew people in this world did bad things, but I never talked to them about the degrees of evil humans were capable of committing. Gianna hated that I never opened up about work, but I couldn't exactly talk about my feelings after questioning a woman who had just cooked her baby in the microwave oven, all because she was hooked on meth.

Seeing that image in my head again made me want to down a straight shot of rum, another one of my favorites to curb the anxiety. My hand began to shake as I thought about work. I shook it off and made a fist, something I had done in the past. Gianna nagged me about my drinking becoming a habit, but it was the only way I knew how to numb the pain. I took a deep breath, closed my eyes, and took in the sounds of chirping cicadas and crickets. I saw a flock of birds settling to their resting place in a swarm to the tops of the tree branches in the distance. I began to feel at peace being away from the city that sheltered the cruelties of humanity.

"Christina!" Vanessa yelled suddenly.

"Christina!" Gianna yelled after her.

"*Christina!*" I heard the shrill of panicked voices as they both called out in unison.

I quickly ran toward the truck and into the open field. And then, it happened. The darkness I thought I'd left behind had followed me here. Something from it came out to play... and swallowed my little, baby girl into the night.

CHAPTER 4

"When did you say you saw her last, ma'am?" the park police asked, with eyes to his notepad, scribbling away. Gianna and Vanessa sat huddled in the cabin clubhouse, sobbing and frozen.

"We've been through this already," snapped Gianna. "We need to gather a search party and go out and *find* her, *now!*"

I reached for Gianna's hand to console her, but she immediately sprung off the long wooden bench inside the cabin's lodge and started pacing back and forth, wringing her hands in front of her. It took close to an hour for the park police to arrive. By then we had already combed the perimeter of the campgrounds with flashlights, several times, alongside campers who offered to help. But there was no sign of Christina anywhere. She seemed to have vanished without a trace.

"We've already placed several of the local authorities on alert," said the ranger. "They're on their way with rescue dogs. No one's allowed out of this park without providing identification first and allowing us to search their vehicle."

"Well, you're not moving fast enough," Gianna screamed, tears in her eyes.

"Look, I'm a father too, folks, and trust me when I say we're doing the best we can. But we need to get all the details first so we can have a good starting to point to help you find your little girl." The ranger seemed concerned. Having been on that side, I knew he was just as eager to want to help us find her.

"*We gave you all the details you needed,*" Gianna yelled and stamped her foot. The officer turned to me and exhaled.

"I'm sorry, mom," said Vanessa. "It's all my fault. I should've kept an eye on her." She drove her head into the inside fold of her elbow and sobbed.

I leaned over and placed the palm of my hand on her back. She didn't spring away with her usual scowl. Her shoulders began to tremble.

"Listen, sweetie. You can't take the blame," I said.

Gianna moved toward her and held her. I never felt so powerless as I did now. "Vanessa, we all know Christina tends to wander off. If anyone can find her, it's your dad. Tell her, David."

Gianna looked at me with her beautiful, big brown, anticipating eyes, yearning for a response. My answer hung on her every breath. I couldn't remember how long it had been that she looked at me with such need. In law enforcement, we were taught never to make such promises to the distraught. But today I *needed* to believe in hope and faith. This was my little girl, and I wasn't going to rest until I brought her back

"I'm gonna find her, sweetie. I promise you that. Mike's bringing a volunteer group from the department to help us find her as we speak. You'll see, honey."

Vanessa and Gianna embraced me, and my girls huddled and cried in my arms. I tried hard to contain the surge of emotion I felt rising from the depths of my chest. I needed to be strong for them, but a light swell of tears trickled down my face. Gianna clutched me tighter.

"It's okay to cry, David," I heard her say. "You don't always have to be the strong one. We're here for each other." They were such wise words in such a small statement, yet, I didn't know why I found it so hard. It was what I was taught. My father taught me that if a man couldn't hold it together, he wasn't a man at all. I had to be the one who protected everyone else from harm. Emotions were weakness, and a man had to find a way to stuff that weakness deep into his soul and make it impenetrable. This had always been my role in our family. I didn't know of any other role to play.

Suddenly, Mike, several of my friends from the department, and several park police officers rushed through the double-wide doors to the clubhouse. The show of support overwhelmed me. I greeted the guys, thanked them for coming, and briefed them on what had happened. The state park officer pulled out a map and discussed the logistics and dangers of the area: caves along the west border of the park, deep ravines and rapids in the southern area, steep hills to the north, and dense untouched pathways to the east. The lodge started to fill with more camping volunteers, and then the canine unit arrived. Everyone kept theorizing that she had wandered off, gotten herself lost, and couldn't find her way back once night fell. It was the most likely scenario. But I wasn't buying it. A horrible, dark anxiety overwhelmed me. I didn't know why or how I knew – call it detective's intuition – but I knew she hadn't wandered off. I needed time to breathe and think on my own, away from everyone else.

I reached for Gianna's hand. "I'll be right back," I said. "I need something from the truck."

She stood on her tip toes and kissed me on the lips. I felt a surge of electricity run down my back.

"Hurry back," she said. She didn't seem as distraught as she was before. Judging by the crinkled lines on her forehead, her expression on her face had gone from one of panic to worry.

As I stepped into the truck, I did what I 'd tell most of my victims after an incident. I needed to retrace my steps, organize in my head what everyone was doing at the exact moment that Christina disappeared. *Lightning bug!* I could recall her shouting, imagining her Supergirl cape dancing freely in the wind as she ran. My beautiful little girl – so innocent, curious, and full of life. I never thought I'd find myself on the other side of tragedy, feeling so powerless, desperate, and panicked all at once.

I gripped the steering wheel and a surge of anger swept over me. Suddenly, I curled my right hand into a fist and brought it down like a hammer, banging over the dashboard several times. I think I heard it crackle and pop. *This couldn't be happening.* Not to my family. Not my little girl. Not today. Not to me. The emotion that started at the pit of my stomach swelled and unleashed itself into a violent wave of frustration, anger, and heartache. My chest hurt. My head pounded. My mouth yearned for a hard shot of tequila, but there was nothing here to numb the pain; nothing here to take my worries away. Suddenly, I stopped. My chest rose and fell into deep breaths. It hurt to feel so broken. So helpless. Suddenly, something shiny caught my eye.

Gianna carried a necklace of a cross on the rear-view mirror. She believed. I didn't. It began to sway in circles. I suppose the movement of the truck as I banged on the dashboard stirred it. Who I was and what I had seen in my line of work always made it difficult to buy the story that a loving God came to die for the scum of humanity. But something compelled me to reach for it. I placed it over my neck. I never had an interest in knowing who He was, or what He wanted from me, but I promised in this moment of weakness and lack of control over my own circumstances, that if He could heal my pain, fix my family, help me find my little girl, I would do everything in my power to get to know who this Almighty Being was and what He wanted in my life. "Please. Help me," I called. *"Help. Me."*

I felt the solid impenetrable wall, that hid my emotions from the world, begin to crack. Perhaps it was the corrosion of pain, guilt, and sadness that had finally worn it down. Out surged a flood of tears. My whole body trembled and my shoulders convulsed. I doubted I had ever cried so hard. Pain. All I felt was pain. And no amount of strength could keep this mere mortal from gluing together all the shattered pieces that exposed my soul and broke me in half.

CHAPTER 5

The cluster of law enforcement officials and volunteers arrived and organized themselves into groups at around 3:30 am. Gianna and Vanessa looked exhausted and sleepy. An aging air conditioner rattled and clanked in the background producing the smell of dank mold in the air combined with the smell of burnt coffee. I was used to the round-the-clock shifts that came with my line of work, and nothing came handier like the acidic burn of what my crew liked to call dark-brewed sludge, which the kitchen staff at the clubhouse supplied. That was enough to keep me up all night. My family, on the other hand, was usually asleep at this ungodly hour.

"Perhaps it's better if you and Vanessa stay behind," I said to Gianna.

"No way," she said. "I'm going."

She wore a dark, stoic expression, with her eyes fixed past me as she glanced into the dense woods. I knew better than to try to persuade her otherwise. Once she dug her heels deep into the sand, that was where they stood. On the other hand, we agreed that Vanessa would stay at home base with the other volunteers who had set up cots with blankets inside the clubhouse. Mike's wife Cindy promised to look after her.

We started with sweeping the open clearing. I could hear the deep *whup-whup-whup* of the rescue helicopter blades above us as two choppers navigated the cloudy skies, illuminating the dense woods with their long-beamed spotlights. If they hadn't gotten here two hours before, Gianna would've gone out looking for our baby herself. There was much to be said about a mother's love for her children. She would put herself in the line of danger if it meant keeping her babies safe, but at a moment such as this, I needed to keep a clear and level head if I wanted to find our little girl.

"The canines picked up a scent," someone called out from the west side of the clearing that bordered the campsite entrance, "I think we have our starting point!" Fifty flashlights darted in that direction. I sprinted with Gianna and a throng of volunteers toward them. I recalled the map and remembered that the west pathways led to natural caverns that bordered that side of the state park about four miles in, followed by denser forest surrounding those caves. I remained hopeful that perhaps Christina had

found her way to one of those caverns and fallen asleep there since she couldn't find her way back.

"The dogs are heading in this direction, so this is where we'll start," pointed the K-9 officer.

I heard a rumbling of thunder in the distance. The sky lit up with flashes of lightning behind us. That rain that we thought was going to beat us when we first came in taunted us with its show of jagged rods of flashes. I feared the worst. The K-9 officer looked at me with concern, and I knew what he was thinking. If the rains came in, that could affect the scent the dogs had found, since new rain had a tendency to wash away the scent and lead the dogs to wherever the water carried it. I hoped that he wouldn't mention that out loud. Gianna didn't need to know that.

"We need to move fast," the officer said. "Stick in groups of four and light your flashlights in every direction along the trail to make sure that you don't miss a single clue. The slightest piece from a hair clip to a tissue could be something that the dogs may have missed. If you find something, say it loud and let us know. Got it?"

The volunteers nodded at once and we began our journey into the woods. The sound of leaves crunching beneath our feet coalesced with the excited yelp of barking dogs. It gave me a glimmer of hope as we walked the trail in silence.

"Hey, buddy," said Mike. "We're going to find her, alright? You'll see." He patted my shoulder with a massive hand and squeezed. I looked back and nodded.

"You think she could be in one of those caves?" Gianna asked, striding alongside me.

"I'm almost sure that's where she is," I assured her. I really wasn't sure, but I couldn't let her see that. I didn't want to add to her anxiety. She grabbed my hand and squeezed it tight.

"I don't remember how long it's been since you did that," I said.

"What?"

"Hold my hand."

"Oh." She let go.

I reached for her hand. "Don't. It's nice." The darkness made it hard to see her expression, but I thought she flashed an uncertain smile.

We walked for forty minutes into the night, with flashlight beams bouncing in every direction. Suddenly, the dogs let out a raucous of loud barking and yelping.

"Stop!" called the lead officer. The officers ahead of us seemed to fixate on the ground. One of them leaned over to reach for something next to a tree, with the dogs still going wild around that area.

"What is it?" I asked.

He turned to us and held up something bright crimson.

"Sir... is this hers?" he asked.

"*Ohmygod!*" screamed Gianna.

I saw the object but froze, unable to speak, for in that man's hands – covered in the crimson color of blood – he held the one thing Christina loved most.

"Sweet, Lord in Heaven," Mike said behind me. Gianna wailed into the crisp night air. And me...well...I couldn't find the words to say that the blood-soaked cape that this man held was the same cape that, just hours before, danced freely in the air while tied haphazardly to my little girl's neck.

CHAPTER 6

At 5 am the dogs picked up a scent past the trail where we found Christina's cape. Five miles later, they led us down a steep slope leading to the caves on the west side of the park. The storm rolled in an hour before dawn, as dark, gray clouds swelled enough to spill over angry daggers of rain that stabbed at every angle before pouring in large sheets. The dogs zig-zagged in confusion as they approached the bottom of the slope, which confirmed my fears. Drenched by the cold rain, the search-and-rescue leader raised his hand and came to a halt. The choppers had vanished as quickly as the lightning appeared. The static call over the team lead's radio told me that they called off the search until the weather improved.

"We can't turn back," cried Gianna, loud enough for me to hear over the pelting rain. The slope was disintegrating into rivulets of thick, slippery sludge around us. I reached for her hand and signaled for her to wait. I felt her cold, damp hand shaking from the rain. We had already traveled deep enough into the woods that it didn't make sense to turn back. We had reached a low gulley. There was a river just south of us that could be swelling fast. I had a bad feeling about this.

"We have to turn back!" cried the search-and-rescue leader.

"*No!*" said Gianna.

"Listen ma'am." He spat on the ground as he spoke. A large bulb of tobacco was wedged into his cheek. "We all want to find her, but these grounds get saturated from the rain right away. It can cause dangerous mudslides and real rough terrain. There's also the rising river just south of us, which tends to flood in a matter of seconds. I can't risk any lives going forward."

"We're not going back," screamed Gianna. "Tell him," she said, nudging me forward.

I scanned our group and saw nothing but raincoat-covered vinyl heads. Beams of flashlights stood frozen as our team waited to see if we were going to retreat or move forward. I knew the importance of needing every single one of those pairs of eyes to help me find my Christina. The thunder and lightning seemed to be retreating, but there was no telling when the rain would subside. I didn't want to postpone the search. We had come too far. On the other hand, we could lose some of our volunteers if we persisted.

"Is it possible to head down to the caves and wait out the rain there?" I asked.

"Negative," he yelled. "Those caves lead to deep caverns for a reason. They're the first thing that floods if the river overflows. We'd be trapped there if that happened. We need to get to higher ground and head back uphill." He pointed over my head.

Time was something we didn't have. I knew the first twenty-four hours of a child's disappearance were crucial to that child's survival. I couldn't back down.

"Well then, you're gonna have to go without us. My wife and I are going forward with or without your help, so step aside."

"David, you're not thinking straight," Mike said behind me.

The team lead smirked and stepped forward. He nodded toward me and grimaced. Rainwater tunneled through his red beard and streamed from it in urgent rivulets. His chest inflated before me in the way of men in positions of authority, seeking to intimidate others into compliance.

"That's not gonna happen," he said. "Everyone goes back together."

I could feel my anger boiling to the surface. I readied myself for a fight, like any battlefield dog would react when pushed into a corner. I was tired, hungry, and sleep-deprived. I shoved him and thrust my finger in his chest.

"I'm gonna *find* my daughter with or without you." A sheet of lightning flashed above, followed by a booming thunderclap. The lightning lit up our carnal rage.

The team lead charged at me, but lost his footing in the mud. He quickly righted himself and edged forward, I stepped toward him in response but felt the restraint of hands on my shoulders and arms.

"Wait a minute, gentlemen!" shouted Mike, stepping between us and shoving an arm into each of our chests. "There might be a way we can gain some ground coverage without necessarily heading all the way back. We can head back uphill and try to wait out the storm there. We'll be at a higher elevation there. We have plenty of tarps and rope we can use to tie to some trees for coverage. We'll have a better vantage point from there to see if the water's rising."

Gianna nodded at him and looked to me. I knew Mike was right. I instantly felt thankful he was here. I began to understand how easy the lines of emotion could get crossed when it was my child now who was missing. My chest ached and tighten in a way I had never felt before. This must be what it felt like when desperation and anxiety mixed itself into a cocktail of toxic worry.

"Sir, you don't understand how fast water can *rise*," barked the search-and-rescue lead. "We're putting everyone in danger here."

"Thirty minutes," I said. "Just give us thirty minutes to wait out the storm. If the rain isn't gone by then, we'll head back."

I held my breath and watched him. There was no way I intended to follow through on that, but I needed time. It was my only ally to help me find my baby girl and bring her home. I couldn't just give it up. The rain continued to pelt the ground around us, but it had let up slightly. I clung to the hope that it would go away. It would be dawn soon, and we'd be able to cover much more ground in the daylight.

The scout lead scanned the hill behind me. "Thirty minutes," he said. "Nothing more. If that rain's not gone by then, we're calling it."

I nodded. Mike patted me on the back. Gianna exhaled a sigh of relief.

We turned and began our climb back uphill. The thick mud beneath us clung like suction cups to our boots. Occasionally, we slipped as we trudged along. Maintaining our balance while holding our flashlights and carrying soaked backpacks made this climb almost impossible. I began to think it was going to take us thirty minutes just to climb our way back. The weight of the rain dissipated, and a trickle of hope crossed my mind. Gianna seemed to be struggling with her climb. I placed my hand on her back for support. She looked over her shoulder and flashed a nervous smile.

"We're gonna find her, David," she said. I was grateful she was beside me, trudging up this hill. It was the only thing keeping me sane. "I can feel it," she said. "We must have faith."

Faith. I thought about it. I didn't really know what that meant. *How could a loving God allow us to go through all this? How could Gianna be so sure?* Having faith was not a strength of mine. I needed some evidence to feel any optimism. I relied on facts. That was how one solved a case. Faith wasn't a part of the equation. I mulled over the idea of faith – how one could be so sure even when there was no obvious reason for it.

Suddenly, I heard a panicked scream. I don't know how it happened. One moment, Gianna was in front of me clinging on to faith, and in an instant, gone. I turned, reaching out to her as she rolled down the side of the wood-covered hill, her screaming voice fading as she disappeared before my eyes.

~*~

I yelled after Gianna but got no response. Like that, she vanished from view, sliding down the darkened slope, behind the pines and out of sight completely. The woods were dark around us. I trembled with fear and froze. By now, the rain had stopped but she was nowhere in sight. I never felt so out of control in my life.

"*Giaaanna!*" Mike bellowed next to me. He had a booming voice that could travel miles ahead, I imagined.

"*Giaaanna!*" I yelled after him. The dogs in front of us seemed to drown out our calls.

I felt relief seeing a sliver of sunlight cut through the pines, as we made our descent down the hill's trail. Maybe now we could navigate our way through the broken branches and track marks she may have left behind as she rolled down the muddy hillside.

"Giaaanna!" I yelled again. Suddenly, I heard a faint voice in the distance.

"Stop. Quiet!" I shouted. The rescue team came to a halt. A cold chill ran down my back in the dead silence of the woods. The morning robins that normally rose to greet the sun had disappeared. *"Gianna!"* I called again.

"I'm here!" she called back, her voice thin and lost.

I shut my eyes and whispered *thank you.*

"Are you okay?" cried the team leader.

"Yes!" she called out. "Something broke my fall. I'm here!"

We rushed downhill toward her voice. I surged frantically ahead of the pack. "Keep talking!" I yelled back. "We're coming!"

"I'm here. It was a mound of leaves that broke my–"

I knew I would never forget this moment. This moment, followed by a blood-curdling scream in the distance. It sent shivers down my back. Her terrified cry carried past those woods in long screams, followed by short pauses that seemed to loop over and over again. I didn't remember anyone following or how my feet carried me there. But I do remember the moment I arrived. Terror was too kind a word to describe the look on my wife's face as her screams pierced those silent woods. In the middle of a small clearing she stared with horror at a pile of leaves behind her. I didn't understand what she was yelling at until I saw it. A face. Or something resembling a face with darkened eyes and the pale skin of a child, hidden underneath that same pile of leaves.

CHAPTER 7

It took two men to pry Gianna away from the crime scene. She didn't want to leave when the help arrived to transfer us on four-wheeled ATVs. She knew our girl was still out there. Lost. Alone. Hungry. But I knew the reality. The worst part about doing my job was telling parents that their child was no longer alive. Convincing Gianna that our child had suffered the same fate at the hands of this monster was no different. Denial can be a powerful weapon when you want to protect yourself from the pain that's splitting you in half. It's not that I didn't feel any pain or want to acknowledge her suffering, I just wanted to disconnect myself from the stages of grief that would soon follow like denial, anger, bargaining, depression, and get to the part where I could hunt this killer down. If anyone was going to grant him justice, that person was going to be me. Only my justice wasn't going to involve screw-headed defendants or lenient judges. Nor was it going to be swift and painless. I wanted it to be Slow. Painful. Agonizing. I'd call that my starting point.

Mike and the search team lead stayed behind to wait for the forensic investigators, who were going to take pictures of the crime scene before the body would be airlifted to the medical examiner. The *body* – I couldn't even say it. Maybe it was shock, exhaustion, guilt, or all of the above, but I couldn't come to terms with giving the body a name – the name of my little girl.

I rode with one of the drivers on the four-wheeler headed back to the clubhouse. Gianna refused to ride with me. I couldn't say I blamed her. I knew I had failed. I looked over my shoulder to see how Gianna was doing. Her blank expression – just the void in her eyes – revealed how broken and exhausted she was. I wondered if I could ever put those pieces back together. A knot formed in my throat, and I brought my hand to my neck to rub down the pain that kept me from swallowing. I could feel the tiny metal chain swinging over my chest as we slid and bumped over the muddy surfaces of the trail. I smirked and stared into the blurring terrain. That necklace had been about as useless as my faith. Something compelled me to reach for it. I wrapped my hand over the little cross clinging to my chest and gripped it so hard I could feel one of its corner edges pierce my skin. I yanked it off my neck, feeling the clasp click as it broke away from me. Anger swelled from the pit of my stomach and I tossed the chain off the trail.

"Hey, are you guys almost here?" shrilled a voice over the driver's radio. It was coming from home base.

"Be there in five, over," said the driver.

"Just thought you guys should know that someone tipped off the media that The Eraser has struck again. We've got that vulture, Jimmie Zack and his maggots, making their way over here already."

"*Dammit!*" I said to no one.

"Just thought you might want to hightail those family members here before they get bombarded with questions, over," said the voice on the radio.

I was fuming. I could read the headlines now: *"The Eraser Strikes Again!* This time, he's taken the child of one of the detectives on the case."* Vanessa didn't know anything. The last people we wanted her to hear it from, first, was the media.

"We need to step on it," I yelled into the driver's ear.

"Ten-four." The driver shifted into high gear and raced ahead. I felt the cold chill of the post-rain breeze penetrating my bones. Each side of the trail was a dark blur of mesquite trees, leaves, and branches.

We pulled into the parking lot of the lodge and I saw Vanessa sprinting toward us. I didn't know what I was going to say. I didn't even know how to put the words together that I needed for her. *Your sister's no longer alive, I'm sorry.* Suddenly, I felt nauseous. The all-terrain vehicle Gianna was riding in pulled up next to us. She had been comatose after her discovery, but the moment she saw Vanessa, she came to life, emerging as the strong woman I'd known for years. She unloaded herself from the backseat of the four-wheeled bike and walked toward

Vanessa. I got out and followed close behind. Vanessa stumbled and froze. She had taken one look at her mother's face and came to an abrupt stop a few feet away.

Silence. We stood in silence, and Gianna began to cry. Vanessa's eyebrows furrowed and her forehead crinkled as her expression transformed right before my eyes from that of hopeful excitement to sheer dread.

"No," she said. "*NO!*" Her head shook and she trembled in place. "*Why her? WHY?*"

Gianna reached for Vanessa, stepping forward with arms extended in an attempt to hold her, perhaps comfort her in her arms, or needing to feel the comfort of her other child.

Vanessa recoiled. "It should've been *ME!*" she yelled.

She turned and ran away from us, sprinting behind the lodge where the open campsite was. Gianna started to run after her, but I reached out and tugged her elbow to hold her back. I lunged and wrapped my arms around her, bear-hugging her. "Let her be," I said as she squirmed to get away. "Let. Her. Be."

"Let her be? That's how you handle all our problems, isn't David?"

I felt the sting of her words and released her.

She turned into me. "Just let everyone be and they'll all fix themselves. Or Gianna will do it for me, huh?"

I was at a loss for words.

"Better yet, how about a good, long *camping trip*- to fix all of our problems?" She yelled as she inched toward me.

I shook my head. I couldn't believe what I was hearing.

"What are you saying?" I spoke softly so as not to attract any attention, but by this time, I could feel eyes peering at us in the parking lot. I leaned in and grabbed her arm to pull her near me. "Are you saying this is all my fault?"

She squinted and pursed her lips. "I'm saying I'm done just letting things be," she whispered darkly. She yanked her arm away and trudged down the same path Vanessa took.

I motioned to go after her before stopping and turning back. Halfway to the lodge I froze and turned to look over my shoulder. She never turned around as she stomped away. Her words cut deep into my soul. I felt resentful.

I wanted to call out for her, but she wouldn't have listened. I wanted to run after her again, but I didn't know what to say. I didn't know what to do. I didn't know how I could help them. I could see my girls hurting and my family coming loose at the seams. I had lost the only person in the world who saw me as a hero. Everything was unraveling into chaos, and there wasn't a damn thing I could do about it. I walked to the lodge and grasped the front door handle. A cold chill ran down my spine in that moment. I contemplated my options: let her be or do something about this.

~*~

A young teenager is rummaging through her tent with tears streaming down her face.

"Where is it?" she calls out. "Where is it? Someone found it in the field. I know it's here."

She tosses a sleeping bag, a pillow, and a pair of shorts over her shoulders. "It's here. I KNOW it is!" she yells again. Suddenly, she sees it tucked into the corner of the tent's entrance. She reaches for it and steps outside. A fallen tree log rests behind a large sage bush concealing it from the open clearing to her campsite. She runs to the log with the item on her hand. She sits on the log and weeps bitterly as she brings a Wonder Woman Barbie doll close to her chest and cradles it back and forth.

"Why did it have to be you?" she cries. "Why?"

The sound of a tree branch snaps behind her. She turns to look and sees no one.

Her shoulders convulse as she continues sobbing. Suddenly, leaves crunch close behind her.

She turns to look. Her eyes widen as one large hand comes toward her mouth and the other puts a vice-like grip around her torso.

She could feel her body lifting and her legs thrashing. Her voice was muted and she trembled with fear, all at the hands of a monster who had caught her in the silence of an isolated area, certain in the absence of witnessing eyes and just at the right moment, when no one was looking.

CHAPTER 8

The victim throws her head back and connects with his nose. "Aaahhh!" shouts the perpetrator, releasing his grip on her.

"HELP!" shouts the young girl. "HEEEELP!" She struggles to pull away as his fingers grasp at her hair and pull her back. Finally, the monster tackles her to the ground.

She feels the full weight of his body on her back, bearing down on her, suffocating her as he wraps duct tape over her mouth. She struggles to scream but her voice is muffled by the adhesive vinyl. Suddenly, he reaches for her wrists. She tries to resist but she's no match for his strength. He turns her to face him and straddles her pelvis. He straps her wrists together with zip ties. His filthy hands rip her T-shirt apart, and she shuts her eyes tight as tears stream down her face, convulsing under the touch of his abrasive fingers. She can feel her hands losing circulation from the tightness of the thick bands. She's scared. So scared. This is real. This is happening. It can't be. Her thoughts scream inside her. No. NO! Please, DON'T! Her eyes widen and every muscle tightens.

Suddenly, two hands grasp him by the scruff of the neck and yank him off the young girl.

A woman shouts, "Get away from my DAUGHTER!" as she tries to reach for a heavy rock on the ground, but he grabs her ankle and falls on her backside. The mother screams.

The young girl clambers to her hands and knees. She tears through the tape and manages to yell, "Leave my mother alone!"

Was there no one around to hear them? Why would there be? The only campers left were the volunteers who chose to stay and help, and they were all back at the lodge. She wants to run for help, but would her mother still be there by the time she got back? The monster straddles her mother's body and throws punches to her face, missing some as she uses her forearms to shield her face, but landing others to her mouth and nose. The young daughter grabs him by the hair to pull him off her semi-conscious mother, but he throws her back with a swift shrug, and she lands in a hard thud. She sees a heavy piece of dead wood next to her and grabs it with her hands tied together. She rises to her feet, ready to swing it full force into his face.

The monster pulls out a switch blade, clicks it open, and edges it to her mother's throat.

"Tsk, tsk," he says.

The young lady freezes.

"You be a good girl now and drop it, or I cut right through her carotid artery and you'll have to stand there and watch."

She looks at the stob of wood in her hands and then at her mother, whose face is crimson red and her lips have ballooned to twice their normal size.

"Don't listen…" her mother attempts to speak as blood streams from her perforated lips.

"Mommy," she cries. Her hands tremble and her shoulders shake.

"Listen to what I'm telling you, young lady. Or you'll have to live the rest of your life knowing you killed your mother!"

"DON'T," her mother repeats. One of her eyelids is swollen shut.

She has no choice. She can't let her mother die. She opens her fingers and releases the heavy wood, which falls to the ground. "There. Now let my mother go please," she pleads, her voice quavering.

The monster's eyes grow dark, like someone has reached in and pulled out his soul, leaving nothing but a void so empty there's nothing anyone can do to stop him.

~*~

I reached for the handle of the lodge door while contemplating Gianna's last words to me: *I always let everybody be…*

I knew that was code for *I was never there for them when they needed me the most*. She had a way of twisting the knife a little deeper, till it cut right through. Her words stung deep. I thought I was doing my job as a father to provide, but I knew my family always needed more from me. Part of me wanted to say to hell with her. If she wanted to leave, let her leave. To hell with trying. But I couldn't, especially now that I had lost my Christina. What type of man would I be if I let them all go?

Suddenly, something bright reflected through my peripheral vision on the left. A flash of light sparked in the far corner of the building, hanging from a hedge in front of the lodge. I released the door handle and stepped toward it. I was shocked to see the same necklace I tossed off the trail. Odd. I turned on my heels and thought of walking away, but guilt took over me. It was Gianna's necklace after all. I didn't need her using this as a weapon in our next argument, so I picked it up and slipped it into my jeans pocket. I turned to walk back to the lodge when something stopped me in my tracks.

I thought I heard a distant scream for help. Call it intuition or that detective feeling that kept me alive all these years, but something told me to check in on Vanessa and Gianna. I broke into a light jog as I headed back toward the campsite. I heard another distant scream and picked up the pace. The words *get away* and *daughter* ricocheted through the trees. It was a yell of distress from a familiar voice. I was always a fast sprinter, but today I carried a speed I didn't know I had. I broke into a full sprint at a hundred yards out from the campsite.

"*Help!*" called out a second voice.

I felt my chest about to burst open as I ran, but I pushed the pain away. I saw it as I drew closer. Past the clearing of our campsite and into the woods stood my Vanessa, staring at the ground. Her T-shirt had been ripped open. I felt a rage boil to the surface that I had never felt before, or perhaps it was already there, but I never wanted to give in to that type of darkness.

Vanessa dropped what look like a thick stob of wood from her limp fingers. Her wrists were zip-tied together. She stood pleading with a man, her eyes stricken with terror. The man straddled a lifeless body and wielded a knife. My eyes widened when I realized the person lying helpless beneath him was Gianna. My beautiful wife, her face covered in a bloody mess as this man – this *monster* – prodded a knife into the side of her neck.

I felt the darkness grab a hold of me and wrap me in a thick blanket of hatred and vengeance. The fabric of my soul unraveled and exposed something raw, cruel, and primeval. The man, who always believed that the laws of justice would prevail, disappeared in an instant. In that moment, my inner monster unleashed itself, bringing with it a reign of fury and wrath on this piece of vile scum who had no regard for human life.

CHAPTER 9

I could see Gianna reaching for his wrist as she struggled under his weight. I raced toward him and lunged with everything I had, tackling him away from my wife.

He didn't know what hit him. He fell heavily and dropped the knife. I rolled over the man and landed on my knees. I looked with panic at Vanessa, who stood trembling.

"Grab it! Get your *mom!*"

I flew into a rage and pinned him to the ground with my chest. He reached for my gun, which was safely secured to my holster.

"Nuh-uh, asshole. We're doing this the *hard* way."

I punched him in the jaw with my left hand and reached for his wrist with my right. I twisted it counter-clockwise with everything I had until I heard it snap. He yelped in pain and spasmed. A sense of power surged through me unlike anything I had felt. I heard Vanessa screaming something unintelligible behind me until the sound of her voice faded. The world was instantly transformed into a dark tunnel. Everything else vanished from focus except for the body beneath me. "You like hurting little girls, do you? *DO YOU?*"

His legs thrashed underneath me as he felt my full weight on his chest.

"You messed with the wrong people, *dickhead!*" I landed another punch, this time to his nose. Blood spattered on the dirt next to him.

"I can't... I can't help it," he said through wheezing breaths. "It's me. I surrender. I'm...the...Erase–"

I didn't want to hear it. I didn't even want to hear his name.

"I don't give two *shits!*" My right fist cracked his nose and cheeks, busting the tissue of his face. I landed several blows in quick succession, lefts and rights, one after the other. The flesh of my knuckles ripped open as they met his teeth. He gasped for air, but nothing was going to stop me from inflicting the same pain he caused my little girl, my family, and everyone whose lives he ruined. My arms grew numb as I pummeled him. His face became a bloody mess, but I wasn't going to stop. He *had* to pay. And I was going to be the one to make him do it. It was time to save the taxpayers some money and give him his sentence right then and there. Without thinking I reached for my weapon and brought it to his swollen lips.

"Open it!" I commanded.

He shook his head and coughed, gargling blood in a foamy, sordid mess, uttering,

"I had to. I had to come back. I couldn't help it. Had to see for myself."

"Open your *damn* mouth or I'll shove this right through your teeth!"

He started crying like a little bitch. He whimpered and opened his mouth, grimacing in pain as he did. I wedged the barrel into it.

"Not the same when it's you feeling the pain, is it?" I had no problem being his judge, executioner, and jury at this very moment. To *hell* with the consequences!

"Dad!" I heard Vanessa screaming behind me.

"David, don't do it!" shouted Gianna.

My hand shook from adrenaline and the weight of my gun. I struggled to catch my own breath, but I wasn't going to stop until he was dead. His red eyes widened and his face strained. He knew what was going to happen next.

I leaned into him so only he could hear me. "You feel that?" I whispered. "That's fear, *asshole*. Same fear you delivered when you tortured those little girls. Including, *mine!*"

His eyes widened again. I wanted to make sure he knew he deserved what he had coming. He closed his eyes and shook his head.

"Only you won't be going where they went when you took their lives, *raped* them, *mutilated* their genitals, and deformed their *faces*. Remember that?" His entire body trembled. Tears and blood streamed down the sides of his face. He no longer looked human, having been reduced to a mass of trembling flesh and fear.

"*STOP!*" said Gianna. "*Don't!*"

I felt her and Vanessa tugging at my shirt behind me, trying to pry me off. But they couldn't. I was a wall of stone. He didn't deserve another day of sunshine on his face, air to breathe, or even one last request. Wolves didn't deserve to walk among the sheep. And we had many sheep with no clue they were about to be eaten.

I steadied my finger on the trigger and released the safety with a loud click. "I'll see you in hell, ass—"

"Daddy? What are you doing?"

But something stopped me instantly. It was a voice, a familiar voice that tugged at my heart at the sound of my name. In my madness, I thought I heard my little girl; my Christina, calling my name as if I was hearing it for the first time. Tears streamed down my face and I shook them off. I swallowed hard, shoving the barrel of my gun further into his mouth. He gagged.

"Daddy, *stop!*"

An image shuffled in front of me. Two tiny feet in gray high-tops stepped into my line of sight. It was Christina, draping a wool blanket over her shoulder. She extended her hand and placed it over mine. She shook her head.

"Don't do it, Daddy."

Was it possible? Could it be? Was I imagining it? I closed my eyes and shook my head. The sting of sweat burned my eyes.

"It's *me*," she cried.

"Put the gun down, David," called Mike from a distance behind me.

I looked up and saw two officers next to him and closing in. Mike held his hands out cautiously as he inched toward me.

"We found her," he said.

"It's over, Detective Johnson," called the other officer.

"Christina? Is that really you?" I asked, my voice cracking.

I saw her doe-brown eyes staring at me, perched above chubby cheeks. She nodded slowly.

"Give me the gun, David," said Mike, holding out his hand to me. "It's gonna be alright."

"Listen to him David," Gianna said from behind me, somewhere out of view.

I looked down at my pistol. The perpetrator held his breath. He closed his eyes. His forehead furrowed as he awaited his sentence.

"It's gonna be okay, bro," said Mike. I looked up at him. "Your family needs you. Now hand over the gun."

"Do it, Daddy," urged my little Christina. My baby. My life.

He didn't deserve to go through the system. He didn't deserve to have anyone run to his defense. He needed to be punished. I took a deep breath and paused. Then, I did what I didn't think I'd be capable of doing at this moment. I removed the barrel from his mouth. The last of his breath escaped as I dismounted from his wretched body. I rose and handed Mike my pistol. The man rolled over as two officers ran toward him to place him in cuffs. Christina sprinted to me and buried her head in my aching heart. All I could do was hold her and cry. A torrent of pain, anguish and relief swelled and spasmed out of my chest.

"Thank God, you're alive," I said. My voice cracked under my cries. I felt chunks of mud and debris in her beautiful, sandy brown hair. I knelt and pulled her in closer. I had no idea what horrors she must have endured with this monster, but I shoved those thoughts away. All that mattered was that she was here, alive, and in my arms. Vanessa and Gianna ran to us and draped their arms over us. We held each other and wept.

"*Christ...ina,*" I muttered through broken sobs.

Her little hands cupped my face and lifted it to meet her eyes.

"It's okay, Daddy. I'm fine."

But how could she be fine? After what he did to that last victim, how was this even possible?

"Where have you been?" Gianna asked.

"I escaped."

"Escape? How?" I asked.

"The bad man took someone else before he stole me away. There were two of us. Daddy, I did a bad thing."

"Bad?" It wasn't possible that this little soul could even think that her actions were bad. Then, her almond-doe eyes looked up at mine.

"When he wasn't looking, I punched him where you said I shouldn't punch you."

Gianna tightened her lips and cracked a laugh.

"Way to go, sis!" cried Vanessa. She raised her hand for a high five.

"I tried to run, but he grabbed my cape and I had to let it go." She pouted her little mouth and her eyes filled with tears.

Gianna leaned into her and wiped them away. "It's okay, honey. We'll get you a new one."

"I was so scared, Daddy, and then your friend found me."

I furrowed my eyebrows, "Mike?"

She shook her head. "The man with the blue cap with the star on it, Daddy."

"Where is he? Is he here, sweetheart?"

Christina shrugged. "He said he had to go away for a little while."

"Where's that, sweetie?" asked Gianna.

She shrugged again.

"Did he hurt you in any way?" I asked.

"No, Daddy. We sang songs and played. I've only been gone a few hours, Daddy. Why are you all making such a big deal?"

Vanessa, Gianna and I glanced at one another with puzzled looks of disbelief.

"Honey, you've been missing for almost two days."

Christina crinkled her nose and nodded. She leaned in and whispered so that only I could hear her.

"He told me to give you a message."

"What message, honey?"

She looked behind her to ensure that Vanessa and Gianna were not listening. She brushed them away with her hand. They looked at each other and stepped back, pretending not to hear. Christina wrapped one hand around my neck. With the other she concealed her mouth as she leaned in and whispered,

"He told me to tell you to remember your promise, Daddy..."

CHAPTER 10

Gianna walked into the bedroom dressed in her spaghetti-strap black tank top and camouflaged silky shorts.

"The kids fell asleep instantly. That helicopter ride must have lulled them to sleep," she said.

She held two glasses of wine in her hands and offered me one. I stepped out of the bathroom, towel wrapped around my waist, and dried my head with another. It felt good to wash the grime of caked-in mud, dirt and blood off me, and to see it vanish down the drain in a black and red swirl. I reached for a glass and set it on top of the dresser.

One of her eyes was covered with a square bandage that covered five stitches and a scratched retina. Her other eye was bloodshot and bruised. The swelling on her lips subsided, and except for a chipped tooth, the rest of her teeth survived. It stung me to know that this creep had no problem inflicting her with that much level of violence, and a part of me wished that I had finished the job. I let out a deep breath as I opened one of my drawers to pull out my shorts, trying to search for something to say,

"Yup, can't thank Mike and his wife enough for driving the truck to the hospital."

She sat at the edge of the bed and placed her glass next to her night stand. I watched her cross her legs and saw the black and blue marks everywhere. I felt a dart of anger radiating through my entire body. I yanked a pair of shorts from my top drawer and winced when the top of my hand brushed against the drawer.

"Ouch!"

Gianna jumped off the bed, drew near me, and reached for my hand.

"You need to bandage these again and add some of that anti-bacterial ointment we have in the bathroom."

"It's okay. I'm fine."

"David Johnson, get in that bathroom right now and let me bandage those hands."

Even through one eye, she wore that passionate, sassy expression I loved about her when she meant business. I gave in to her demand.

"Fine, but only 'cause you're giving me the pirate death-stare, and it's really intimidating right now."

She followed behind and stepped in front of me. She placed her hand on my abs and began to run her fingers through my chest hair. Startled and intrigued, I looked at her with one eyebrow raised. Suddenly, she balled her fingers to capture the hairs around it. "You better take that pirate comment back right now, or I'm yanking."

"No, no, NO! I take it back. I take it BACK!" My hands went up in the air.

"Say you're sorry," she demanded.

She raised the one eyebrow I could see. Although I could only see one eye, I saw the same fire I fell in love with when I first met her. Her expression exuded passion, determination, and strength. I missed that so much during the times when I only saw defeat, exhaustion, sadness. I couldn't help but feel like I had had something to do with that. My smile disappeared, and a lump formed in my throat. I cupped my hand over her closed fingers and took a deep breath. I wasn't used to being forthcoming with her, but something told me I needed to let it all out.

"I'm really sorry, Gianna. For everything."

I saw her exhale and stare into the ground.

"You've done so much for this family," I said, "and not *once* have I ever truly thanked you or expressed gratitude for your hard work." I could feel her fingers loosen. "I've taken you for granted, but I've realized just how important you are to our kids and my life."

I paused and waited for her to say something. But she was quiet. Her uncovered eye looked glassy.

"I know you had dreams of your own that you gave up to support mine, and I know there's nothing that I can do to change that. I promise you this. If you're willing to keep trying, I'll dedicate the rest of my life to making sure I do everything I can to support you in any way I can."

She looked pained. A tear trickled down her face. I wiped it away with the back of my fingers. It pained me to see her cry. It pained me even more to know I caused it.

"I have to go into work Monday morning to turn in the report, and I want you to know that I plan on withdrawing my promotion as lead detective and applying for a desk job. It's not too late for you to go back to school. Administrative work will allow me to be here for the kids more, and I can help out around the house."

"No," she said. She stared into the ground.

Panic set in. "Please hear me out, Gianna," I pleaded.

She shook her head. "No," she repeated.

"But I can't live without you, Gianna."

She looked into my eyes. "No, you can't quit being a detective."

I took a step back. Was this a test? Was this one of those things where she says no, but she's really checking to see if I choose the secret, right answer behind the magic door labelled *you better get this right*?

"No?" I asked, puzzled.

"I've never regretted being here for my family, but I never expected to be going at it alone, either, much less also giving up the things I wanted to do because of it. I needed a partner."

"I know."

She exhaled slowly. "I also believe all of this crazy stuff happened for a reason. It made me realize you were made for this line of work as much as you were made to be a good provider, father, and a husband."

"But I failed you on the last two."

"You still have the rest of your life to make up for it, just like I still have the rest of my life to pursue an identity of my own."

"What are you saying?"

She drew nearer. Her hand reached for my jawline. "We'll figure this out together, as a family. After what we've been through, there's nothing that says we can't all work toward achieving a common goal we can all be happy with. But I need to know we're all in this together. Because at the end of the day, all that really matters is our family and the love we show each other. How we treat each other is far more important."

I breathed a sigh of relief and began to cry in front of her, something I didn't like to do. "Sorry," I said.

"Don't apologize for feeling pain," she said, wrapping her arms around me. "It's okay."

I held her. I squeezed her so close I thought I might break her. "I'd die for you," I said, my voice cracking.

"I know," she whispered. She pulled away and her lips dove into mine. She tasted of red wine and strawberries. My hands ran down her back, the side of her hips, and then slid to her back side, squeezing and drawing her near me. I lifted her and placed her on the double sink vanity, sliding my lips down the side of her neck. She let out a soft moan. Her nails ran lightly down my back, which drove me into a frenzy of heavy breathing. I nibbled lightly on her shoulders.

"I love you, David," I heard her whisper. She reached for the tucked-in portion of my towel with impatient hands.

I heard it drop to the floor in a heap. I tugged and pulled down her silky, pajama shorts almost desperately, yet delicately to avoid touching her fresh bruises. It was hard to do when all I wanted was to devour her, consume her in one breath.

"I love you too," I said.

My tongue ran down her beautiful breasts and she moaned again. Her fingers traveled to the back of my head and tugged hard at my hair. We were caught in this moment of frenzied excitement. She scooted to the edge of the counter, allowing me to enter and accept the snug warmness of her invitation. She wrapped her legs around my waist. "I've missed you," I said. She pressed her lips delicately against mine and kissed me with a passion I hadn't felt in a long time.

I lifted her up in the air and stepped out of the bathroom, with her strapped to my hips. We fell into the bed, savoring each moment. Intoxicated by her smell, I took in the softness of her skin as I wrapped myself in the embrace of my beloved wife. She moaned. I cried. She cried. I moaned. I took in her goodness, her mercy, the purity of her heart, and felt it cleanse my soul. We had been travelling one journey on two separate roads in the last seventeen years, but tonight it felt like a forked road had finally converged into one. I couldn't wait to find out what walking on that same road would feel like. Tonight, I

BETWEEN THE WOLVES AND THE SHEEP

was her beloved and my beloved was mine. I felt filled with hope and gratitude as I was reminded of the promise I made in that truck back at that camp, during a moment filled with pain and despair. It was a promise I intended to keep for the rest of my life.

CHAPTER 11

I walked into the courthouse at peace with what I was about to do. Nestled to the right, back corner of this small building, I stepped in to the administrative office. Rectangular in shape and divided into two parts, the right side was filled with the sounds of printers scanning, people typing, and staplers pounding as the civilian workers processed court documents at their desks. Toward the back of that room stood a steel door that led to a long running corridor that opened into another building housing the offices of the sheriff and the deputy chief. The left of the room was divided by a wall in which the top half was part bullet-proof glass that ran up to the ceiling, and sustained by a bottom half of white-painted concrete that ran down to the floor. The area on the other side of that glass, housed the entrance to the new-and-improved booking department. I shook my head in disbelief. New policy regulations designed to make things more transparent and community-friendly now required criminals coming from the court magistrates to be booked within full view of all civilians visiting the administrative building. This was a liability waiting to happen, but politicians wanting re-election didn't care to listen to the opinion of the actual grunts who had to deal with the real criminal element.

The booking office didn't seem as chaotic for a Monday, but judging by the female booking officer's look of disdain, I guessed she wasn't happy with the new arrangement. I walked up to the long wall-to-wall counters that divided the lobby waiting area from the civilian employees.

"I'm here to speak to the chief," I told the front desk assistant, a woman named Martha.

She smiled and picked up her receiver to let Bethany, the Chief's administrative assistant, know I was here for my appointment.

With the Eraser finally captured, I spent a lot of time contemplating what I was about to do. I was surprised by the fact that I had no regrets. I knew I had Gianna's support with whatever I decided. On the other hand, I also knew that I needed to be present for my family. The one thing I regretted in life was the time I missed with my girls that I was never going to get back.

Bethany walked from behind the steel door. She wore black heels, a tight pencil skirt, and a red, ruffled, low-cut blouse. Her eyes and dark lashes laser-beamed right at me.

"The chief is caught up in a conference call, gorgeous," she said, "but he'll be out soon."

She leaned into the counter, unafraid of displaying her gifted assets in full view.

"Can I get you a cup of coffee, handsome? Or anything else you may need?"

She played with her hair. "No thanks."

My eyes traveled to the left, where I saw a small group of prostitutes, drunks, addicts, murderers, and rapists waiting to get booked. It was unusual for a Monday after a weekend of waiting for the courts to open. It was a smaller crowd than usual, as if few had gotten together and decided to take the day off.

Bethany reached for my left hand and squeezed it, as she leaned in and whispered,

"Everyone here can't stop talking about catching The Eraser. You're a hero now. If there's anything you need, Detective Johnson, you give me a ring, you hear?"

I withdrew my hand. I didn't know if it was the blatant disregard for the fact that I was married, or that I had a teenage daughter only six years younger than her. Maybe it was just the continuous innuendos she kept throwing out, but something told me that it was time to draw the line.

"Listen, young lady, because I'm only going to tell you this once..."

She threw me a surprised look and took a step back.

"You see this ring? Whether, you think I'm happy or not, it means I'm committed to someone. You may have no clue what that means, but it means I belong to someone else. If you respect yourself enough, you'll understand that you deserve so much more than another person's leftovers. If you don't, and are comfortable with being someone else's second helpings, please move along to the next poor sap, 'cause this fish isn't going to take the bait. Have I made myself clear?"

"Ugh," she scoffed as she looked around the room. "Easy there, tiger. You're not the only fish in the sea, and I've got plenty of nets."

"Is that so? Well then, please take your fishy, smelling nets and cast your traps elsewhere."

"Your loss." She snapped her teeth, turned in a huff and stormed off.

One of the desk clerks behind the counter waited for her to go inside the chief's office. She glanced over to me and threw me a silent applause and a thumbs-up, mouthing the words 'well done.'

I shrugged and turned toward the front desk assistant.

"Going next door, Martha," I said. "Let me know when he's ready?"

Martha nodded.

I stepped into the booking office to see two inmate trustees mopping the waiting area in front of the high leveled counter where the booking officer sat. They lectured one of the inmates who was about to get processed. No matter how much they mopped this area, the smell of ass, armpits, and urine was overwhelming. I could never get used to this smell.

"Possession of a controlled substance, child endangerment, and prostitution all in one arrest?" Officer

Jefferson scolded. "Woman, what the *hell* were you thinking?"

The inmate's eyes opened wide. "Who the hell are you to judge? You don't know my struggle. You don't know how hard it is."

I knew Officer Jefferson. This conversation was not going to end well.

"Oh *hell's, no!* Wait a minute. Stop right there. You want to talk struggle? My momma raised five kids on her own in a neighborhood where not even the Po-Po wanted to go, and crack was available in every freakin' corner block you walked to. They were giving it away like candy. Our version of the YMCA was joining a gang in that hood, missy, so don't you tell me I don't know your struggle, because we come from the same stock... mmm-hmm"

The inmate rolled her eyes and looked away. "Fuckin' Uncle Tom sellout," she said under her breath.

"*No.* No, don't do that! You look at me when I'm talking to you, young lady. Do you know why I'm here and you're there? Choice. This is your third offense, and you chose to not get your ass into rehab the first time the judge got you off. Instead, what'd you do? Oh yeah, you got high on meth, while your kid was getting raped in the next room. So, don't you address me that way, you *stupid* bitch, 'cause now you've made it even harder for that young child of yours to get through life."

"*Go to hell,*" said the prostitute.

"You, first. Oh, wait. What was I thinking?" Jefferson chuckled. "You're already here. Now get the hell out of my sight before I throw your *bitch ass* out there myself. Officer Lee, get her processed and put her in the holding cell. I don't want to *see* her face."

The woman glared at her.

"Move it," said Officer Lee as he yanked on her arm and took her behind the steel door leading to the processing room.

"Hard day?" I asked.

"Boy, it's only just begun. Why can't I get normal people, like unpaid child support or DWI's?" She shook her head as she rummaged through the pile of paperwork. "Congratulations on capturing that scumbag, serial rapist," she said with a sincere smile. "We were all praying for you, honey."

One of the trustees moving the chairs raised his head in my direction as the other one continued mopping.

"Couldn't have done it without the department's help and the number of volunteers who showed up. Which begs the question, has he gotten processed yet?"

"Not yet. Just got released from the hospital this morning. He's meeting with the judge right now as we . . . well, speak of the devil, look who just walked through the door."

I turned to see a shackled man in a red jumpsuit with handcuffs and leg irons. Our eyes met and he lowered his gaze to the floor. Something inside me wanted to draw my weapon and fire it, but I restrained that urge.

"Look who decided to finally grace us with his presence. Serial Chester molester and rapist, John Wendell

Hornsby, finally captured for the deaths of missing children. Glad to finally meet your acquaintance, asshole. Welcome to my dungeon. Have him wait in the holding cell until we're ready to get him processed," commanded officer Jefferson.

The trustees stopped in mid-mop, glanced at each other, and then turned toward him and glared. The detention officer opened the steel door leading to the holding cells as he ushered him in.

John Wendell Hornsby. Finally, a name to add to the face. Hornsby looked over his shoulder and grinned at me. There was a void in his eyes that made my skin crawl.

Suddenly, one of the trustees behind me shouted, "Hey, what you looking at, Holmes?"

"Alright, alright, get him outta here," yelled Officer Jefferson. "He's even getting on the other inmates' nerves now."

Hornsby turned away and shuffled toward the entrance.

"That's right, *vato*," called the other trustee as Hornsby disappeared behind the door. "You keep moving, Holmes. We'll catch you later."

"You know those two trustees heard what he was getting charged for," I told Jefferson.

"Oh, did they? Whoops!" She covered her mouth sheepishly and winked. "I completely forgot they were even here. Well, I hope news doesn't travel down the grapevine that their guest of honor has arrived. I wouldn't want the welcoming committee to get him settled with the proper accommodations." She laughed and nodded her head. "If they do, things are about to get a lot more interesting for this sick bastard. I just *love* me some karma," she squealed, clapping her hands in the air.

Perhaps she was right. Even criminals lived by a certain moral code that one just didn't cross. Raping and killing children was usually one of those you didn't step over. I felt strangely comforted.

"So...speaking of news, words out that they're going to give you that detective lead. Are you taking it?" asked Officer Johnson with probing eyes.

I could see Martha, the assistant in the other room, flagging me down to let me know that the chief was ready to see me. I winked at Officer Jefferson and stepped into the hallway feeling at peace with what I was about to do. I reached for the door that led into the administrative office as someone else was coming out. We accidentally bumped into each other.

"Whoops, pardon me," the man said. He was a wall of a man, even taller than Mike. He hovered over me with broad shoulders, and deep blue eyes set thick under bushy brown eyebrows.

"No worries," I said.

"Hey, you're that detective who caught that rapist, aren't you?" He crossed his arms and smiled.

"Yes," I nodded and sighed, hoping he wasn't part of the media. I wasn't ready to join the circus frenzy that revolved around this case.

"Your daughter? Is she doing better?"

"Detective Johnson, the Chief's ready to see you," said Martha as I held the door open.

"Yes, yes, she's recuperating nicely," I said dismissively. I waved to let Martha know I was on my way.

"Good. Good. You let her know that I knew she'd be okay," the man said. He reached for something in his back pocket. "I hope she gave you the message."

"Oh sure, okay, no problem," I said and nodded automatically as I slipped through the door. A second later I froze. *What did he just say about a message?*

"Detective," called Martha.

"One second, please." I rushed out the door and saw that he was no longer there. I spotted him in the distance walking past X-ray machines fifty feet away. He looked back toward me and doffed a blue cap. The cap displayed a large gold emblem on it. It was a star of some kind. I squinted and saw it, the Star of David. I waved for him to stop, but he simply smiled and waved again before disappearing behind a crowd of people exiting the door.

I hope she gave you the message... I replayed his words in my head. It was clear as day. Those were the same words my daughter told me he said on the day he saved her. I smiled. *Yes, I got it*, I thought. *Loud and clear.*

THE END

EPILOGUE

County Sheriff's Detective Unit, Indoor Hanging Rafters

"*Why are you here, Azrael? You know it's-s-s... not our time, yet,*" hissed the creature.

"*HE determines the day and time. What makes you think you know that now is not it?*"

The creature stared intently with black, unblinking eyes—"*Because... we all know that it will take more than just one of you to corral us-s-s-s... all. I do, however, have two questions-s-s: What brings the Angel of Death to my neck of the woods-s-s?*"

"*Checking in on someone. But he seems to be leaving early to be with his family, so I see my job here is done. Second question?*"

"*I want to know why you cheated?*" *it asked, as its tongue flickered.*

"*Need I remind you that I answer not to vile beings? But if your curiosity burdens you so, the reason is thus:* He asked and it was given to him; he sought and it was found; he knocked and the door was opened."

"Ah yes-s-s, the loophole."

"Loophole?"

"You can interfere if you wish, should the unbeliever promise to seek a relationship with and live in obedience to the Great I Am. That's a little s-s-self-serving, don't you think?"

"And offering wealth, power and success to serve yours, isn't? The Great I Am requires only love and devotion, while yours demands eternal bondage and damnation."

"We both know that's not the way it happens-s-s. Humans are arrogant enough to invite us in at the cost of their own soul. All they must do is give in to the seven. That's-s-s our opening."

"So, this last one who took the lives of those little girls, which mortal sin did you use to trap this one, Lust? Wrath? Envy? Or did genetics offer you a weakness to be exploited?"

"Does it matter, Azrael? You s-s-saved your man, and we got ours-s-s. And speaking of ours-s-s, I've got a 2 o'clock with a meth addict about to hang herself in her cell. I wouldn't want to disappoint her if I wasn't there for, you know, a little immoral s-s-support."

"Do not flatter yourself, demon. She still has free will."

"Ah, that pesky little free will. Hate to break it to ya, but nope, this one's-s-s a goner. There's hardly anything there left of the Spirit for her to make that decision. It's

pretty crowded, in fact. A legion of us-s-s have had free room and board there for months-s-s when she decided to expand her mind with the wonderful world of mind altering enhancements-s-s."

"The drugs, then. She opened a portal with them."

"Of course, portals into a person's s-s-soul are so much faster and efficient than the usual props-s-s. You know, Ouija boards and séances are so passé. Wouldn't you agree? Drugs-s-s on the other hand, are like toll roads with direct access to the S-s-spirit."

"There will come a time when none of you will have anything left to inhabit with your darkness, fallen one."

"Well, for now you know the drill; where there are those who carry the light in them, there is also darkness-s-s present, wanting a way in. When they create an opening, the light cannot dwell with the darkness-s-s, so the light leaves and the s-s-soul is ours to keep. So why don't you stick to saving your pitiful humankind, and I'll s-s-stick to enslaving them."

"Enough! Your foul presence offends even my tolerant nature. Depart, or my brethren and I will smite you."

"Tsk, tsk, tsk. No need to call for back-up, I was just leaving. Like I said, I have an appointment to keep. Oh, but before I leave, I have one las-s-s-t thing. You may think your job is done, saving that Justice-Seeker down there, or as your humans like to call him, David, is it? But the Boss-s-s thinks he's a threat to our kind. Just know that our job with him has only just begun."

"Is that a threat?" asks Azrael.

"Just letting you know that you better hope he's-s-s as strong as you think he is."

The demon turns into a thick blanket of black before vanishing into thin air. Something is hiding behind one of the vertical rafters. Four angels, beautiful and much smaller than Azrael, like the size of children, emerge from behind it. Azrael's demeanor changes immediately when he sees them.

"Did you all hear that?" he asks in a fatherly tone.

"Yes, Azrael. We did."

"Are you sure you want to do this?"

"We're positive," they say in unison.

"Is that him? Is that the one who caught the one who hurt us?" she asks, pointing to a handful of people below the rafters.

A man is checking his watch and putting away files in his desk.

"It is. It's not going to be easy. You heard. He's been marked."

"We know, Azreal."

"Very well. So, let's begin. What's rule #1 to being a Guardian Angel?"

"Let your person choose," says one.

"Rule #2?"

"Leave signs. Guide, don't push," says the other.

"Excellent, and Rule #3?"

"We must never let him see us, Azrael. Except for his little girl. The little ones can always talk to us."

"Wonderful," says Azrael, as he reaches over and pats one of them on the head.

"You think he's going to make it?" asks one of little ones.

"I don't know. I guess it will all depend on whether he will survive the trials."

"Why?"

"Because it will be up to him. The choice will always be his."

ABOUT THE AUTHOR

Jax Cortez is an indie author, blogger, and freelance writer. She is happily married to her crime-fighting husband and lives in the Lone Star State with her rambunctious tween, who has enough energy to power a whole town. She loves to write stories that empower the unempowered. To read more of her novellas and short stories visit: www.amazon.com/author/jaxcortez

www.ingramcontent.com/pod-product-compliance
Lightning Source LLC
Chambersburg PA
CBHW070641130626
46555CB00006B/2642